Praise for Brian Brackbrick and the Hazard of Harry Hatman

"This is a really good book with adventure and mischief lurking round every corner. I really enjoyed the book because you never know what's about to happen. When they come out, I can't wait to read the other books." (Solomon, aged 9)

"This book is brilliant. I bought this book for my grandson – he absolutely loved the book and to be honest so did I. We can't wait for the next one." (Kevin, a grown-up)

"Brian Brackbrick is an <u>awesome</u> book...I'm so excited for the next book in this series! Well done!" (Archie, aged 9)

"I thought it was awesome and I really enjoyed it. All the characters were fun and I liked George Bum." (Jake, aged 6)

"A lovely, easy to read book for younger readers wanting something a little bit longer." (BB Taylor, a grown-up on the outside)

Brian Brackbrick and the

Mystery of Mrs. Blumenhole

Book 2 of 6

ISBN-10: 1720767416

ISBN-13: 978-1720767411

For DYLAN, OLLIE and OWEN

Every day there is more to
learn, and you are my teachers.

People!

Brian Brackbrick

George Bum

Mrs. Blumenhole

Fancy Nancy Sprinkle

Dr. Harley Letters

Frankie Featherface

Harry Hatman

Mr. Sparker

Places!

The New Hat Shop

The Flower Shop

The Library

The Cake Shop

Things!

A Woolly Hat

Southern Dripping Red
Nettle Plant

Very Rare Giant Purple Spotted
Tonic Bush

Eastern Mini Squirt-Ball
Orange Fruit Plant

ALSO BY THE AUTHOR

Brian Brackbrick and the Hazard of Harry Hatman

PREVIOUSLY...

Brian Brackbrick and George Bum discovered that Old Mr. Hatston from the hat shop had disappeared!

In his place was the very strange Harry Hatman, in a very different hat shop.

Harry Hatman used a mind-controlling bowler hat to take control of Brian's dad Mr. Brackbrick, until

George Bum bravely saved the day with a well-aimed cupcake.

Harry Hatman seemed to be working for the mysterious 'Mr. Sparker', but no-one knows who this is.

Meanwhile, Old Mr. Hatston is still missing...

CHAPTER 1:

THE NEXT DAY

Brian Brackbrick was very worried about Old Mr. Hatston.

Yesterday, Brian Brackbrick and his best friend George Bum had had a rather eventful day.

Harry Hatman had been arrested and taken away, and all his special hats had been confiscated by Sergeant Shelley Shiplap (well, all except for one woolly hat, which she had missed…).

They had both been given medals, and everyone had cheered, but still, no-one knew what had happened to Old Mr. Hatston. Brian Brackbrick hoped that he was okay.

As he was the one-hundred and thirty-eighth cleverest person in the world, Brian Brackbrick was quite sure that he would be able to work out where Old Mr. Hatston was…

…but, it was much too noisy in the house this morning to think clearly.

Mrs. Brackbrick (Brian's mum) was busy doing all the housework, and she liked to sing while she worked. She would sing really old songs very loudly, and, Brian suspected, with all the wrong words.

Mr. Brackbrick (Brian's dad) was adding to the noise by making lots of very boring work calls on the telephone.

If only there was some way for Brian Brackbrick to cut out all this noise so that he could think clearly…

The singing suddenly stopped. Mrs. Brackbrick called from downstairs, "Brian! Is this one of your hats? It looks very cosy. Would it fit me?"

She had found the woolly hat from Harry Hatman's shop, with all the twiddly bits and flashing lights inside. It could still be dangerous!

Brian Brackbrick ran down the stairs and snatched the woolly hat before Mrs. Brackbrick could put it on.

"Goodness me, Brian," said Mrs. Brackbrick, who was rather flustered. "Whatever is the matter? It's only a hat!"

"Yes indeed, only a hat, ha ha," laughed Brian Brackbrick. "I did not realise I had left it there. Thank you!"

Brian Brackbrick tucked the hat under his arm and ran back upstairs to his room, leaving a rather puzzled Mrs. Brackbrick staring at her suddenly empty hands. He quickly packed the woolly hat into his backpack, and put on a tartan cap (as he would never leave the house without wearing a hat). Perhaps there was a way to make the woolly hat safe, and solve the problem of a noisy house at the same time…

That was for later, though. For now, Old Mr. Hatston was still missing. To find him, Brian Brackbrick needed the help of his best friend – George Bum!

CHAPTER 2:

WHERE IS

OLD MR. HATSTON?

Brian Brackbrick walked two doors down to George Bum's house. The front door opened just as he reached out his hand to knock. George Bum stepped out of the house and quickly closed the door.

Brian Brackbrick's house may have been too noisy sometimes, but George Bum's house was a million times noisier.

George Bum had five younger brothers, and a huge smelly dog called Slobberchops.

His younger brothers were called Jack and James, Bob, Jeff, and George Two (their parents had run out of names by that point).

Brian Brackbrick wondered how George Bum could think at all in all that noise and chaos.

"Where are we going today, Brian?"

"There is a mystery to be solved," answered Brian Brackbrick. "We must find Old Mr. Hatston, and make sure he is alright. Someone needs to run the hat shop, after all!"

They walked along the main street towards the hat shop. A big truck was parked outside the pet shop, where Frankie Featherface worked. Two men were unloading crates and boxes in front of the shop.

On the side of the truck was written:

Brian Brackbrick thought this was strange, because Frankie Featherface usually only sold animals that were soft, cute and cuddly – he was terrified of anything else.

The dirt on some of the crates reminded Brian Brackbrick of the previous day's events, when they had encountered Harry Hatman in the bright and shiny new hat shop.

"I was thinking, George – when we were in the hat shop yesterday, it was bright and very clean, not a bit of dust or dirt anywhere."

"Yes, I remember," said George Bum thoughtfully. "Not all dusty like when Old Mr. Hatston was there."

"Except – the petals and bits of leaves on the floor!" declared Brian Brackbrick. "Those petals and leaves can only have come from one place!"

"Yes, Brian," agreed George Bum. "Remember what Fancy Nancy from the cake shop told us about Old Mr. Hatston?"

"We will get to that, George. I think those petals are a clue to where we should look first!"

"That's right, Nancy said that – "

"In a moment, George," interrupted Brian Brackbrick. "I must tell you where those petals and leaves came from!"

"They came from Mrs. Blumenhole's flower shop," said George Bum patiently. "Remember, Nancy said she saw Old Mr. Hatston going into the flower shop, and no-one has seen him since."

Brian Brackbrick was quiet for a moment. "Oh yes. Nancy did say that. Well then, let us go to the flower shop!"

On their way they passed the hat shop and stopped to look in the window. It was closed, locked up, with no lights on. It was very sad to see it closed up and empty.

"We must find him, George," said Brian Brackbrick. "Let us see what Mrs. Blumenhole has to say," and with that, they pushed open the door of the flower shop and went inside.

CHAPTER 3:

STRANGE PLANTS

IN THE FLOWER SHOP

The flower shop was called:

Precious Petals and Dazzling Displays of Brilliant Blooms for All Occasions

The inside of the flower shop was a blaze of colour, with plants and flowers from every part of the world.

It was always very hot inside, like the jungle or the rainforest, sometimes with steam in the air if the plants had just been watered.

Mrs. Blumenhole kept it so hot because of all the tropical and exotic plants and flowers she had in the shop.

Mrs. Blumenhole had worked in the flower shop for a very long time, since she had been young Miss Petal. She liked to wear a mix of green and brown clothes, and so she often faded into the background behind the colourful flowers and plants.

The boys walked in to the flower shop, and Brian Brackbrick's glasses steamed up straight away as usual. Mrs. Blumenhole was watering some of the plants, with a sad expression on her face. Usually Mrs. Blumenhole was happy and friendly, but she was different since Old Mr. Hatston had disappeared.

"Hello, boys," Mrs. Blumenhole put down her watering can and tried to smile. "Are you here to buy a bunch of flowers?"

Brian Brackbrick shook his head. "Actually, we would like to ask – "

"A nice bright pot plant for the garden?" interrupted Mrs. Blumenhole.

"No, thank you, Mrs. Blumenhole," replied George Bum.

"Some red roses for a lucky young lady?" Mrs. Blumenhole tried again.

Both boys looked down at the floor. George Bum had gone quite red in the face.

"Not today, thank you, Mrs. Blumenhole," said Brian Brackbrick. "We wanted to ask you some questions."

"No time for questions, boys," Mrs. Blumenhole picked up her watering can and turned away. "I have to take care of all these new plants and flowers. I've had to put them all in pots, prune them, feed them, and water them."

The plants and flowers Mrs. Blumenhole pointed out did look very colourful and exotic, even for a flower shop that was called:

Precious Petals and Dazzling Displays of Brilliant Blooms for All Occasions

Some of the leaves were unusual shapes, and the stems and branches twisted around in strange ways.

"We need to ask you about Old Mr. Hatston," said George Bum.

Mrs. Blumenhole stopped for a moment, sighed, then pretended not to have heard. "I have to take care of these new plants and flowers. They are all needed for the pet shop."

"Why does the pet shop need plants and flowers?" asked Brian Brackbrick.

"Well, the new animals will need plants for food, and for their habitat. You know, to eat, live on, hide behind, and all that," explained Mrs. Blumenhole. "They are very...fussy, I think. Very choosy about what they need."

Mrs. Blumenhole pointed to a small pot plant with orange-coloured fruit. The fruit was very tiny, but looked like it was incredibly juicy. "Like this one, the Eastern Mini Squirt-Ball Orange Fruit Plant."

Mrs. Blumenhole then pointed to another small plant, with rough-looking dark green and red leaves. The leaves were covered with beads of oozing liquid, and there was a very strong smell of cheesy socks coming from it. "Or this one, the Southern Dripping Red Nettle Plant."

"What about this big one, Mrs. Blumenhole?" asked George Bum, pointing at a large plant with purple-spotted leaves.

"That one?" said Mrs. Blumenhole. "Oh yes, that one might come in handy…"

"What do you mean, Mrs. Blumenhole?" asked Brian Brackbrick.

"Never mind. That's enough questions for today," said Mrs. Blumenhole.

"What about Old Mr. Hatston?" George Bum tried again.

"No more questions! Too much to do! All these plants for the pet shop!" Mrs. Blumenhole sniffled as if she wanted to have a good cry.

"Let us go, George," whispered Brian Brackbrick. "We do not want to upset Mrs. Blumenhole. I think we need to find out more about these special plants. To the library!"

CHAPTER 4:

DR. LETTERS EXPLAINS

THINGS ABOUT PLANTS

Brian Brackbrick and George Bum walked into the library to see Dr. Harley Letters dusting the high bookshelves. The shelves were so high he needed a ladder to reach them.

"Hello there!" Dr. Letters shouted down. "How are you two doing after all that unpleasantness with Harry Hatman?"

Charlie Chipchase was there, sitting in a comfy chair and reading a book with his usual frowny face. "Do you mind?" he complained.

"We are fine, Dr. Letters!" Brian Brackbrick called out, ignoring Charlie Chipchase.

"Why don't you come down from the ladder, so we don't have to shout?" shouted George Bum.

"What a great idea!" yelled Dr. Letters as he climbed down the ladder. "Now, what can I help you with today?"

"We would like you to tell us about some plants," said Brian Brackbrick.

"Plants?" asked Dr. Letters.

"Yes, plants," said George Bum.

"Mrs. Blumenhole has some strange new plants in the flower shop, and we would like to know more about them," explained Brian Brackbrick.

"Ah, I see! In that case, follow me! Knowledge awaits!"

Dr. Letters led them through the library. (He knew every book and shelf in his library, and could always find what you were looking for right away.)

They eventually reached a shelf labelled Exotic Plants and Flowers from Around the World.

"Do you know the names of the plants?" asked Dr. Letters.

"Of course!" replied Brian Brackbrick, who was the one-hundred and thirty-eighth cleverest person in the world, after all. "The first one is called the Eastern Mini Squirt-Ball Orange Fruit Plant."

"Hmmm, let's see," Dr. Letters said thoughtfully as he looked along the shelf. "This one, I think." He selected a book called Orangey and Lemony Plants of the World and opened it up on a desk so that they could all see.

The page had photographs of the plant they had seen in the flower shop, and other plants like it. Some were big, some were small, some had tiny fruit, and some had huge hanging orange fruit that looked bigger than the rest of the plant.

"These are all the different types of Squirt-Ball Orange Fruit Plant in the world," explained Dr. Letters. He pointed to one of the photographs. "This one is the Eastern Mini Squirt-Ball Orange Fruit Plant."

"That is the same as the plant in the flower shop," said Brian Brackbrick.

Dr. Letters read out loud from the book. " *'The most interesting feature of this plant is the tiny fruit, which is irresistible to creepy-crawlies, especially scorpions. Scorpions just cannot help themselves, and will ignore everything else to get to this fruit.'* "

"Scorpions!" exclaimed George Bum.

"It would seem," said Dr. Letters, "that this is a rather clever plant."

"What do you mean?" asked Brian Brackbrick.

"Well, this plant uses the tiny fruit to **attract** the scorpions to it. Lots of plants do this, you know. Some will attract birds, which eat the fruit and then scatter the seeds. Some will attract things like ants or other insects, which protect the plant in return for food or shelter."

"Things like ants – or **scorpions!**"

"Yes indeed, George," agreed Dr. Letters. "Now, what was the next plant?"

"It is the **Southern Dripping Red Nettle Plant,**" said Brian Brackbrick.

"Ah, yes, that will be an easy one." Dr. Letters chose a book called A Guide to Nettles and

Stingers and opened it up. "Here we are, is this it?" He pointed to a photograph that looked exactly like the second plant they had seen in Mrs. Blumenhole's flower shop.

"Yes, that's it," said George Bum.

Dr. Letters again read out loud from the book.
" '*This type of nettle plant does not sting people at all. The leaves are covered with a thick liquid which smells of old cheesy socks. Creepy-crawlies do not like this smelly liquid, especially scorpions, which will never, ever go near it.*' "

"Scorpions!" exclaimed George Bum again.

"Another clever plant. It seems this one uses the liquid to repel, to keep away the creatures it doesn't want, who might otherwise eat the whole plant."

"Interesting," said Brian Brackbrick.

"Now, what was the next plant?" asked Dr. Letters.

"We don't know the name of the last plant," said George Bum. "Mrs. Blumenhole didn't tell us."

"Well, that's a shame. Can you describe it?"

"It is large," explained Brian Brackbrick, "more like a bush than a pot plant."

"The leaves are very wide, and they have big purple spots on them," added George Bum.

"Purple spots, eh? I wonder…" said Dr. Letters, reaching over to the shelf and taking a book called Poisons and Venoms and their Natural Antidotes. He opened it up on the desk. "How about that one?" he asked, pointing to a photograph on the page.

"That is it!" Brian Brackbrick pointed excitedly at the picture.

"This one is called the Very Rare Giant Purple Spotted Tonic Bush. The book says the leaves of this plant can be used to make you better if you are stung by a scorpion."

"Scorpions!"

"Just one type of scorpion, George," explained Dr. Letters, "called the Very Rare Purple Spotted Scorpion."

"This is all very strange," said Brian Brackbrick thoughtfully. "Mrs. Blumenhole said she has all these new plants for the pet shop, but Frankie Featherface does not like scorpions, or any creepy-crawlies."

"Remember the truck outside the pet shop, Brian."

"Yes, indeed, George."

They were interrupted by Charlie Chipchase. "Will you stop talking so loudly about scorpions and trucks and plants? Some of us are trying to read quietly!"

"Just in time, young master Chipchase!" said Dr. Letters quickly. "You can help me put away these books! Oh, and these as well," he said, pointing to a huge pile.

"Let us go, George," said Brian Brackbrick. "Perhaps we should visit the pet shop!"

Brian Brackbrick and George Bum left the library, leaving a very annoyed Charlie Chipchase behind.

CHAPTER 5:

FRANKIE FEATHERFACE

IS VERY BUSY

Outside the pet shop, Brian Brackbrick and George Bum saw that the truck was no longer there, but there were lots of boxes and wooden crates on the pavement. Standing there amongst them were Frankie Featherface and Lord Mayor Spencer.

They seemed to be arguing about something.

Lord Mayor Spencer walked off, leaving Frankie Featherface standing outside the pet shop looking rather cross.

"Good morning, Mr. Featherface," said Brian Brackbrick.

"Hmm? Oh, hello, you two," said Frankie Featherface.

"What's in all these boxes and crates, Mr. Featherface?" asked George Bum.

"Ooh, I don't think I can stand to even talk about it." He looked down at the boxes and crates, and then quickly looked away in disgust. "Awful, awful things."

Both boys bent down to look at the boxes and crates. They all had labels on. One label read:

Another said:

HORNED SPIKY
TERROR LIZARD

Most of the boxes had stickers that said:

DANGER!

...or:

POISONOUS ANIMALS

Every box and crate also had a label that read:

DELIVER TO
MR. CARL SCORPION

"Who is Mr. Carl Scorpion?" asked Brian Brackbrick.

Frankie Featherface shivered. "Carl Scorpion is coming to work with me in the pet shop. He starts tomorrow. So I have to spend the rest of the day sorting out these horrible things."

"But you don't like insects and creepy-crawlies and things like that," said George Bum. "You've never had them in your shop before."

"I know, I know," replied Frankie Featherface, who didn't seem very happy about this at all. "We're going to have a party tomorrow to celebrate all these...creatures. You'll come along, won't you?"

"Of course," answered Brian Brackbrick.

"Definitely," added George Bum, whose family had bought Slobberchops the dog from Frankie Featherface. (Then, he had been a tiny, cute, fluffy puppy. Slobberchops was now bigger than George Bum and all his brothers.)

"Nancy will be making cakes for the party, of course," said Frankie Featherface. He waved across the road to the cake shop. Nancy smiled and waved back, nearly dropping her tray of cupcakes.

Brian Brackbrick and George Bum also waved at Nancy, thinking that there might be some free cupcakes for them (they had saved the cake shop from the Yoghurt Inferno, after all). Nancy's smile grew even wider and she beckoned them over.

"We will see you tomorrow, Mr. Featherface," said Brian Brackbrick.

"Goodbye, Mr. Featherface," said George Bum.

They left Frankie Featherface staring in disgust at the boxes and crates, and headed over to Nancy's cake shop.

CHAPTER 6:

FANCY NANCY'S

HERBAL CUPCAKES

Brian Brackbrick and George Bum opened the door to Nancy's cake shop and walked in.

"Good morning, Nancy!" said George Bum.

"You're just in time, boys!" Nancy smiled as she picked up a tray from the counter. "I want you to try something for me." The tray was full of cupcakes (of course), but they were unusual colours, and were not covered in icing like Nancy's cupcakes usually were.

"What flavour are they, Nancy?" asked Brian Brackbrick.

"They are my new **herbal cupcakes.** You can help me choose which flavours to sell in the shop."

George Bum frowned. "Herbal cupcakes?"

"Yes, I wanted to try something different," explained Nancy. "Each one has a different herb or spice flavour. All made with plants from Mrs. Blumenhole's flower shop. Will you try them for me?"

Everyone knew that Nancy could put anything – no matter how ridiculous or crazy – into a cake. She was an excellent cake-maker. The best around. Sometimes, though, she decided to put things into a cake that really didn't belong there.

The boys also knew that Nancy was quite sensitive, and they always tried hard not to hurt her feelings.

Brian Brackbrick picked up one of the greenish cupcakes, and took a bite. It tasted like medicine and reminded him of throat sweets that were supposed to clear your nose when you had a cold.

"That one is flavoured with eucalyptus leaf," said Nancy, proudly. "Just the thing for when you have a cold."

"It is...interesting, Nancy," said Brian Brackbrick, trying to look like he was enjoying the cupcake. It wasn't really horrible, but it was not the right flavour for a cake!

George Bum picked up a cupcake that had red flakes running all the way through it, hoping that the red bits would be fruit. He took a great big bite. "It's quite nice, Nancy. It's – " Suddenly his face turned bright red and he started to cough and splutter. "Water! Water!"

"Oh dear," said Nancy, giving him a glass of water. "That one is my quite hot chilli pepper cupcake."

George Bum drank the water straight down and his face slowly returned to normal. "That is very hot!"

"Well, I suppose I still have some work to do with these herbal cupcakes," Nancy sighed. "You've been very helpful, though. If you can think of any other plants that I can use, you let me know!"

"We will, Nancy," promised Brian Brackbrick.

"Now, I need to start making all the cakes for the pet shop party tomorrow afternoon. Will I see you there, boys?"

"Oh yes, Nancy," said George Bum. "Especially if you are making the cakes!"

Nancy smiled. "Bless you, boys! See you tomorrow, then."

Brian Brackbrick and George Bum left the cake shop and rushed home for lunch. They wanted to get rid of the taste of Nancy's herbal cupcakes, as fast as they could!

CHAPTER 7:

BRIAN BRACKBRICK

DOES SOMETHING

VERY CLEVER

Brian Brackbrick and George Bum went home, and Mrs. Brackbrick made sandwiches.

Mrs. Brackbrick was upset to hear about the boxes and crates of creepy-crawlies being delivered to the pet shop. She was even more frightened than Frankie Featherface, especially of spiders and scorpions.

"Well, I don't think I'll be going to the pet shop again!" she said. "I should give this 'Mr. Carl Scorpion' a piece of my mind, whoever he is! Anyway, there's plenty of sandwiches for you both, I'm off to the shops!"

Before they started on the huge plates of chunky sandwiches, Brian Brackbrick thought again about the woolly hat, how to make it safe, and how to solve the problem of a noisy house. He selected three heavy books from his bookshelf and carried them to the kitchen table. (George Bum chose some comic books about Captain Awesome, which were packed full of exciting action.)

As they ate their sandwiches, Brian Brackbrick quickly read the first of the three books he had chosen. It was a study book called:

George Bum, meanwhile, was enjoying the comic books about Captain Awesome and his heroic struggles against his many enemies.

He had just got to the part where Captain Awesome is hypnotised by Dr. I. Diddit, when Brian Brackbrick put down the first book.

"Hmm," Brian Brackbrick murmured thoughtfully, and he picked up the second book, which was a science book all about sound and noise called:

George Bum carried on reading the comic books. He had just got to the part where Captain Awesome's most terrible and deadly enemy **Baron Goldpants** reveals his true identity, when Brian Brackbrick put down the second book.

"Interesting," said Brian Brackbrick. He picked up the third book, which was a book about electronics called:

A GUIDE TO CHANGING AROUND "TWIDDLY BITS" SAFELY

BY D.I. WISAFE

George Bum carried on reading the comic books. He had just got to the part where the unpredictable

Captain Chaos turns all of Captain Awesome's friends against him, when Brian Brackbrick put down the third book.

"George, I have got it!" he said as he reached into his backpack and took out the woolly hat from Harry Hatman's shop and a screwdriver.

"What are you doing to the woolly hat?" asked George Bum.

"Sometimes, it is just too noisy to think properly," Brian Brackbrick explained as he poked around inside the woolly hat. "If I could just think quietly for a moment, I should be able to work out where Old Mr. Hatston is."

"Well, you are the one-hundred and thirty-eighth cleverest person in the world, after all."

"Exactly, George! Now, Harry Hatman put lots of wires, flashing lights and twiddly bits inside this woolly hat. I can change around the twiddly bits to make it do what I want! There!"

"What does it do now?" asked George Bum.

"Try it on and see!" said Brian Brackbrick, holding out the woolly hat.

George Bum put on the woolly hat, and pulled it down over the tops of his ears. It was rather comfy, and warm, but it didn't seem to be doing anything.

Then George Bum looked around. Brian Brackbrick seemed to be talking to him, but there was no sound!

He tried to say, I can't hear you! But he couldn't hear himself speak, either!

He clapped his hands together. No sound.

He clicked his fingers. Still nothing.

Brian Brackbrick looked very pleased. He also looked like he was saying something. George Bum had no idea what he was trying to say, so he took off the woolly hat.

"This is amazing! I couldn't hear a thing with this woolly hat on!"

"That is what I have been saying, George! I have changed around the twiddly bits inside the woolly hat so that it completely blocks out sound! Total silence for whoever wears the woolly hat!"

"So now you can think quietly!"

"Yes, indeed!" said Brian Brackbrick, taking off his tartan cap. "I will figure this out in no time." He put on the woolly hat, and his face became calm and thoughtful.

George Bum carried on reading the comic books. He had just got to the part where Captain Awesome is saved by the people who were his true friends all along, when Brian Brackbrick stood up and took off the woolly hat rather dramatically.

"George, I know where Old Mr. Hatston must be!" exclaimed Brian Brackbrick.

"Where, Brian?"

Brian Brackbrick put his tartan cap back on, and shoved the woolly hat into his backpack. "Mrs. Blumenhole has known all along! To the flower shop!"

CHAPTER 8:

MRS. BLUMENHOLE

SAYS SORRY

Brian Brackbrick and George Bum left the house
and **hurried** to Mrs. Blumenhole's flower shop.
They ran straight past the hat shop, which was still
locked up, empty and dark.

As they burst through the door of the flower shop,
they **surprised** Mrs. Blumenhole.

"Oh, you startled me!" exclaimed Mrs.
Blumenhole. "Are you back to bother me with

more questions?" Her eyes were red and puffy, like she had been crying.

"What is all this for, Mrs. Blumenhole?" asked Brian Brackbrick, pointing at the plants and small sacks near the counter.

"Oh, these are all for the pet shop."

George Bum walked over to look more closely at the plants, and realised that they were small potted versions of the three plants she had shown them earlier.

He then peeked in the small sacks, and saw that they were full of leaves from the **Southern Dripping Red Nettle Plant** and the **Very Rare Giant Purple Spotted Tonic Bush,** and the small orangey fruit from the **Eastern Mini Squirt-Ball Orange Fruit Plant.**

"Never mind the plants, Mrs. Blumenhole," said Brian Brackbrick. "You must tell us where Old Mr. Hatston is!"

"Yes, all for the pet shop," Mrs. Blumenhole mumbled, as if she had not heard. "I must get all the plants ready…or…or…"

"Or what?" asked George Bum kindly.

"Mrs. Blumenhole!" Brian Brackbrick was becoming rather cross. "I have worked it all out! You must tell us where Old Mr. Hatston is!"

"I **don't know** where he is!" shouted Mrs. Blumenhole, who then started to sob. "I'm so worried about him!"

George Bum took a tissue from behind the counter and gave it to Mrs. Blumenhole. "What have you figured out, Brian?"

Brian Brackbrick explained…

"Old Mr. Hatston was last seen coming into this flower shop. Then he simply disappeared! Yesterday, Harry Hatman had taken over the hat shop, and all the hats and hatboxes had vanished! The new hat shop is very clean and bright, very clean indeed, Mrs. Blumenhole. Except for one thing!"

Brian Brackbrick paused. "Except for the petals and leaves on the floor near the counter! I think that those petals and leaves came from this flower shop! You have hidden Old Mr. Hatston!"

"I'm sorry, Brian, but that's not what happened,"
Mrs. Blumenhole sniffled.

"I think you will find that it is what happened,
Mrs. Blumenhole." Brian Brackbrick looked
rather pleased with himself.

"Why don't you tell us about it, Mrs. Blumenhole?" suggested George Bum.

"Mr. Hatston came in to say good evening, like he does at the end of every day," Mrs. Blumenhole said as she wiped her tears with the tissue. "I went out to the back room, just for a few minutes, then when I came back, he'd gone, and there was a terrible mess everywhere."

"Then what happened, Mrs. Blumenhole?" asked George Bum.

"Well, I looked outside," she continued. "He was nowhere to be seen. Then I noticed a load of new plants, which I hadn't ordered, on the pavement outside the shop. There was a note with the plants," Mrs. Blumenhole said quietly, her voice trembling.

"What did the note say, Mrs. Blumenhole?" asked Brian Brackbrick.

She pulled out a piece of paper from her apron pocket and handed it to Brian Brackbrick, who opened it up so that they could all read it.

The note said:

Dear Mrs. Broomhilda Blumenhole,

Greetings to you, I hope you are feeling wonderful on this splendid day in our lovely town.

I have borrowed your friend, the delightful and very interesting Mr. Hatston.

You must grow and take care of all these lovely plants, so that you can supply the pet shop with the leaves and the fruit for all the marvellous new animals.

Mr. Hatston will be completely safe and will have a super fun time while you do this work for me.

Please deliver all the leaves and fruit to Mr. Carl Scorpion, then Mr. Hatston will be returned to you.

Mr. Carl Scorpion will be happy to answer any questions you may have.

Have a wonderful day,

Your friend,
Mr. Sparker

Brian Brackbrick waited for George Bum to finish reading, then handed the note back.

"So you see, I really don't know where he is," insisted Mrs. Blumenhole.

"You should have showed us the note straight away," suggested George Bum kindly. "We would have helped you."

"Yes, I should have," agreed Mrs. Blumenhole. "You boys did stop the Yoghurt Inferno after all! I suppose I just panicked."

"I am sorry, Mrs. Blumenhole," said Brian Brackbrick. "You are not to blame. But, I believe I do know where Old Mr. Hatston is. I believe that

Old Mr. Hatston has been in the hat shop all along!"

"But we can't get into the hat shop," said George Bum. "It's locked, and empty, and all the lights are off."

"I have a spare key." Mrs. Blumenhole pulled a shiny silver key from another apron pocket. "I've always had a spare key."

Brian Brackbrick and George Bum stared at the shiny silver key in astonishment.

"Then there is no time to lose!" declared Brian Brackbrick. "To the hat shop!"

CHAPTER 9:

THE RETURN OF

OLD MR. HATSTON

Brian Brackbrick, George Bum and Mrs. Blumenhole quickly walked next door to the hat shop. Using the shiny silver key, they unlocked the door, which gave off an eerie creak as they pushed it open and slowly stepped inside.

It was **very dark** inside the hat shop, with thick wooden blinds covering the window, but the open door let in just enough light for them to see. They could see the outline of the counter, and the thick shelves that Harry Hatman had put up along the wall.

"We need to find the light switch," said Brian Brackbrick as he fumbled along the wall.

"I think it's behind the counter somewhere," said Mrs. Blumenhole. "As long as the door doesn't close behind us, we'll be able to find it."

There was a creak and a click as the door closed behind them.

"Now I can't see anything!" George Bum bumped into a shelf along the back wall.

"I cannot see anything either!" Brian Brackbrick nearly tripped over a mop and bucket, causing a clattering that echoed around in the dark.

Mrs. Blumenhole kept moving slowly towards the counter, with her arms outstretched. She felt her way around and reached up to the wall. "The switch is somewhere around here," she muttered to herself. As she reached out, all three of them heard another creak as the door opened, and dim light came back into the shop.

None of them wanted to turn and see who had opened the door. Was it Mr. Sparker? Had Harry Hatman escaped from the police station?

A voice called out: "Evening all! What's going on here, then?"

They all breathed a sigh of relief. It was only **Sergeant Shelley Shiplap!** Surely she would help them?

"Thank goodness you are here, Sergeant Shiplap," said Brian Brackbrick.

"It looks like I'm here just in time to prevent a burglary!" Sergeant Shiplap switched on her torch as the door closed behind her.

"We're not burglars, Sergeant Shiplap," explained George Bum. "We're rescuers!"

"Rescuers, eh? A likely story!"

"It's true, Sergeant Shiplap," said Mrs. Blumenhole, who finally found the light switch. They all blinked as the bright lights flickered on. "We are searching for Mr. Hatston."

"Mr. Hatston is not here. I searched this shop myself! I think you should all come with me to the police station! Let's go, come on!"

Brian Brackbrick was just about to explain what had happened, when a **loud groan** echoed around the shop.

"Did you hear that?" asked Brian Brackbrick.

"Yes, I did," said Mrs. Blumenhole.

"It came from the back room!" added George Bum.

"It doesn't matter!" said Sergeant Shiplap. "You have still broken into the hat shop! I have to take you to the police station!"

"We didn't break in," said Mrs. Blumenhole. "Mr. Hatston gave me a spare key."

Sergeant Shelley Shiplap looked surprised. "Oh! Why didn't you say so?"

Another groan drifted from the back room; it sounded like someone in distress…

"We must investigate the noise, Sergeant Shiplap!" insisted Brian Brackbrick.

"Oh, very well then. But I'm telling you, he's not here, I searched this place myself!" They followed Sergeant Shiplap as she walked into the back room. "See? Nothing but piles and piles of boxes, which couldn't possibly be hiding anything."

Brian Brackbrick now knew what had happened to Old Mr. Hatston's hatboxes, and the boxes filled with hatboxes. They were all here, crammed into the back room, piled on top of each other right up to the ceiling. There were gaps between the piles of boxes, just big enough for the two boys to squeeze through.

"Come back here, you two!" shouted Sergeant Shiplap.

"There is no time to lose!" Brian Brackbrick called out, his voice muffled by all the boxes.

They worked their way through the maze of boxes, climbing over and crawling under and squeezing through. They heard another groan, and knew they were close.

"Over here!" called Brian Brackbrick.

There was a big, scattered pile of hatboxes, right at the back of the room. Another groan seemed to come from right underneath the boxes!

They moved some boxes out of the way, and saw first a **hand**…then an **arm**…then another arm…then, the familiar face of a kindly old man!

"**Old Mr. Hatston!**" Brian Brackbrick said with excitement as they helped him to sit up. "You have been here all along, hidden away!"

"Ah…hello boys," muttered Old Mr. Hatston in a rather weak voice. "Thank goodness you found me, I'm so very grateful. How long have I been here?"

"Long enough, Mr. Hatston!" said George Bum. "What happened?"

"Well, I was tidying up for the evening, when I thought I heard someone come into the shop. Before I could say anything, all these piles of boxes collapsed on top of me, and I couldn't move! As I lay there, it felt like more and more boxes were being piled on, and I could hear voices…but perhaps I dreamt that part."

"Perhaps not, Mr. Hatston," said Brian Brackbrick, "but never mind that now. We are so pleased that we found you! Now you can put the hat shop back just the way it was!"

Old Mr. Hatston smiled. "I think…I would like that very much."

CHAPTER 10:

BRIAN BRACKBRICK AND

GEORGE BUM RECEIVE

ANOTHER MEDAL

Later that day, all the people of the town gathered at the front of the library to watch as Brian Brackbrick and George Bum were presented with another medal each by Lord Mayor Spencer.

Old Mr. Hatston was there in the crowd, standing arm-in-arm with Mrs. Blumenhole. Both of them were smiling.

Frankie Featherface was there too, and he was also happy, his worries about the pet shop forgotten for the moment.

Lord Mayor Spencer placed medals around the necks of Brian Brackbrick and George Bum, and everyone cheered and applauded.

"Here we are again, oh yes, giving thanks to young Brian Brackbrick and young George Bum, ho ho," announced Lord Mayor Spencer. "It seems that every day, you two youngsters are going here and there and doing heroic things! Every single day, ho ho."

Lord Mayor Spencer paused for a moment.
"Let me see, so far you have…saved us all from the Yoghurt Inferno…stopped Harry Hatman, who at this moment is safely locked up in our police station…and now you have rescued Mr. Hatston! How wonderful! Ho ho.

Let us have more cheers and applause for Brian Brackbrick and George Bum!"

Brian Brackbrick and George Bum were very pleased to get another medal. George Bum could see, though, that Brian Brackbrick was doing a lot of thinking.

Brian Brackbrick was thinking:

What was so important about all the new animals for the pet shop?

What might happen at the party for the pet shop's re-opening?

Who was Carl Scorpion, and how was he connected to the mysterious Mr. Sparker…?

FIND OUT

NEXT TIME!

BRIAN BRACKBRICK

AND GEORGE BUM

WILL RETURN!

IN...

BRIAN BRACKBRICK

AND THE SCOWL

OF THE SCORPION

COMING SOON!

A WORD FROM

BRIAN BRACKBRICK

Thank you for reading all about my adventures, and I hope you enjoyed this latest story.

I do hope you will join me and George next time? Together we will meet Mr. Carl Scorpion, and find out what is going on at the pet shop!

A WORD FROM

BRIAN BRACKBRICK

The mysterious Mr. Sparker does seem to be planning something. I wonder when we will find out who he really is...?

If you would like to send me a message, please do!

A WORD FROM

BRIAN BRACKBRICK

You can email me –
brianbrackbrick@gmail.com
– or message me on social media:
@BrianBrackbrick (Twitter)
Brian Brackbrick (Facebook)

See you next time!

Brian Brackbrick

ABOUT THE AUTHOR

GR Dix is a scientist in his day job, and a writer of children's books at all other times! He is a late starter as an author, but has been a fan of books, comics and reading his whole life.

The major influences on his writing are (in no particular order) Roald Dahl, Simon Furman, Stephen King and Terry Pratchett.

An active member of the Society of Children's Book Writers and Illustrators (SCBWI), he attends events, conferences and critique meetings as much as possible.

GR Dix lives in the UK, and credits his success to the unfailing support of his wife, family and network of close friends.

You can contact GR Dix through his Facebook page (GR Dix Author), where you can find the latest news and updates.

Printed in Great Britain
by Amazon

27752158R00079